I0567677

THE VAMPIRE'S RESCUE

SHAWN WISEMAN

TABLE OF CONTENTS

1. MISSING FANGS

"Well, the bad news is you're going to need surgery if you want a proper replacement," an older gentleman said.

"Damn," Olivia swore. "There's no other way, Gideon?"

"I'm afraid not," he replied. "Unless you want to back down on the denture option."

"No way am I wearing dentures. I'd rather have only one fang than dentures."

Kara, who was watching nearby, laughed at the prospect of seeing Olivia in dentures. "C'mon Liv, they're not that bad. You're getting along in years," Kara began.

"Getting along in years?" Olivia shouted.

"And there's no shame in needing dentures for a vampire at your age," Kara finished with a devious grin.

Olivia gave Kara a menacing look and pointed at her. "You'd better watch it, Kara. I'll show you who's old." Olivia turned her attention back to Gideon. "So, what goes into the surgery?"

"What we'll be doing is creating what we call a fixed bridge. The teeth surrounding your missing fang will be cut down, and you'll end up with three replacements: the two on the sides will be built back with crowns, and they will support the fang in the middle. They'll be cemented in for stability, but it's not going to be like your old fang. You have to be careful when using them. If you're too rough it could cause nerve damage in the supporting teeth. If you have to drain live prey you should knock them unconscious first, otherwise if they pull away with enough force they'll take your fang with them."

Kara cringed at the thought. The prospect of dentures was looking more appealing, but Olivia seemed undeterred. "Olivia, how about you have a normal replacement? You still have one natural fang left."

Gideon nodded. "That is a possibility, and would be a good alternative for your dental health. And, while I'm not sure if it's the same nowadays, back in my day it used to be a status symbol to have a tooth missing from a psychic. It meant they were afraid of you enough to do some damage."

Olivia glanced from Gideon's bespectacled look of pride over to Kara's concerned smile. She let out a sigh. "Alright, I guess I'll just get a normal tooth replacement."

Kara let out her own type of sigh and then smiled more genuinely. Gideon also smiled as he pulled two plastic molds off the table. "Excellent! I'll just take these molds and we'll get you a temporary set of dentures in the meantime." Olivia was about to object, but Gideon held up his hand. "You need these to protect your gums and exposed teeth, Ms. Lucerno. Do not argue about this one. It's only temporary."

Olivia pursed her lips, and after a nod Gideon left to get some dentures made. She got up from the dentist chair and Kara handed her her jacket. She put on and fixed her hair.

"To think I have to live with only one fang for the rest of my life."

"However long that will be," Kara added.

Olivia shook her head in disgust. "If I ever see that detective again, he'll regret even leaving me with one fang."

"If only I could teach you telekinesis. I can't come to your rescue all the time."

"I'll just make sure to knock him out before he knows what hit him," Olivia replied while flexing her arm. "Are you going to have Gideon check out your fangs as well?" she asked.

"You know I hate everything to do with dentists. All the poking and prodding and picking." Kara shuddered as she tongued her incisors. "I can't stand it."

"You're a vampire too, Kara. You should take care of your assets."

"I'll pass," she said with finality. She pointed to Olivia's pocket. "I think you got a text while you were being examined."

Olivia pulled out her phone and checked her messages. "Looks like Vasha has another assignment for me."

"Mind if I come with you? I have a few hours to kill. Maybe I can help."

Olivia wrinkled her lips and thought it over for a moment. "I suppose," she replied.

Kara laughed at her friend's expression. "You suppose," she echoed.

The Vampire's Rescue

Gideon entered the room again with a plastic denture fitted to a metal wire. He handed it to Olivia. "Here you are. You can schedule with front desk on having the surgery when you're ready."

"That was quick," Olivia commented as she stared at the denture.

"The wonders of three-dimensional printing," Gideon replied with a smile.

Olivia put the denture into place, fixing the hole in her teeth with a new, normal-looking tooth. She turned to Kara. "How do I look?" she asked with a smile.

"Great!" Kara responded. "Now, let's go get you a walker and we're all set."

Olivia stopped smiling. "Not funny," she said before walking out of the room.

Kara laughed as she followed Olivia out to the front desk. Olivia set her next appointment, and the two left the dentist's office. They headed to Vasha's restaurant to see what job she wanted Olivia to take on next.

They entered the restaurant to see it packed to the brim with customers. For the first time, Kara saw the restaurant when it was open, and it was at the tail end of their lunch rush. On the right side of the rectangular restaurant loud patrons enjoyed their food at packed tables, and on the left side diners and drinkers occupied all the bar stools. At the entrance, a female maître d' waited to greet new guests or, this close to closing lunch out, to turn them away.

"Hi Olivia, are you here to eat today?" she asked in a pleasant, friendly tone.

"No, I wish. I'm here to see Vasha," Olivia said.

"Ah," the maître d' replied with a nod. "She's in the back office," she said with a habitual wave of her hand meant to direct customers.

"Thanks," Olivia said, walking towards the back. "You're probably glad I'm not here to eat, it looks busy," she commented, glancing at the bustling customers.

"There's always a table for you, Olivia."

Kara and Olivia weaved their way past customers and staff towards the back of the restaurant. The smells of the food invaded their senses, whisking them away to a realm of fine dining that made their mouths water.

"Is she one of us?" Kara asked.

"No, Vasha employs a lot of normal humans as well."

Kara winced. "Maybe I should be more careful with what I say around here. You've never told me much about how Vasha works."

Olivia laughed. "Yeah, if you're going to be around more often it might be a good idea to watch what you say."

Kara's face reddened and she pulled her hoodie up over her head to hide her embarrassment.

The two of them went into the back office hallway and knocked on Vasha's door. "Come in," Vasha said from inside the room. Olivia opened the door and stepped inside, with Kara behind her, hoodie still drawn.

The small office they entered had a few cabinets, a desk with a computer, and some chairs to sit in. It would be cramped if it wasn't so immaculate.

Vasha was sitting in a comfy leather chair behind the desk. She was wearing a tight-fitting deep blue dress that showed off her curves. Her long, black, wavy hair was tied in a braid and went down the front of her shoulder, contrasting with her blue dress and accentuating the shaved side of her head. She was as stylish as ever, with various rings and jewellery adorning her body.

"Kara, to what do I owe the pleasure of your company?" Vasha said immediately with a snakelike tone.

"I was with Olivia for her visit with Gideon," she replied.

Vasha nodded, then looked at Olivia. "That went well, I presume?"

"Yes—" Olivia started, but then frowned. "Well, as well as can be expected. I'm going to have a bridge put in, but because of possible issues with a fang I decided to get a normal tooth replacement."

Vasha smiled a twinge. "Gideon would suggest that," she chuckled. "He is a man in love with the past, and with old traditions. Nevertheless, it will suit you." Vasha turned her attention back to Kara. "Now, Kara, be a dear and give us the room?"

Kara's jaw dropped and she glanced from Vasha to Olivia and back. Vasha's commanding voice caused her feet to move before her conscious mind objected. "I'm here to help Olivia with her job, if that's what this is about."

Vasha raised her brow. "You are free to do as you wish, provided that you understand this doesn't nullify the favour you owe me. You didn't forget about that, now did you?"

4

The Vampire's Rescue

Kara frowned. "No, I didn't forget. I still owe you; I just wanted to help Olivia."

Vasha smiled. "Good. I might have need of your psychic powers soon," she said with a tone that sent a chill up Kara's back. "Down to business then." Vasha reached inside a drawer of the desk, pulled out a file folder, then handed it to Olivia. "A human scientist, Dr. Anne Barker-Wilson, went missing recently. I need you to find her and bring her back here. In the file it has her contacts and current address. She has a teenage daughter who can give you more details on the kidnapping."

Olivia opened the file folder and skimmed through the contents. Kara looked over her shoulder to see a picture of a woman in her late thirties in a white lab coat. There was a variety of information located within: where she was working, her family and friends accompanied by pictures of each, as well as other miscellaneous data points.

"Got it, I'll report back when I find something," Olivia replied, and then she rose from her seat.

"Woah, wait a second, Liv. Aren't we going to get any more information on this before we leave? Like, why was this scientist kidnapped? What were they working on? Why are we trying to help a human scientist? Is this going to be dangerous?"

Kara glanced back and forth from Olivia and Vasha while she asked her questions, uncaring of the looks each of them were giving her. Olivia's clenched teeth and her rosy cheeks indicated anger and embarrassment, and Vasha's leaning back in her chair and resting her hand on her chin showed that she was holding in her ire.

"That's not how it works, Kara," Olivia replied.

"All that you need to know is in that file," Vasha stated as she leaned forward and folded her hands in front of her face. "If you want to enter this world, you need to learn the rules. Your first lesson is that any job I give you will be dangerous. If you can't accept or handle that, my young dear, then perhaps the wrong person lost her fang."

Vasha's eyes pierced like a sharp cut, and Kara's mind went numb. She felt that she should be embarrassed, but anger was quick to replace the feeling. "I understand," Kara said before she left the office.

Olivia followed behind Kara, and the two exited the restaurant. "What the hell, Kara? You just made me look like a fool in front of Vasha."

Kara shook her head, the embarrassment and anger still coursing through her. "I know, I'm sorry, but that woman is going to get you killed one day," Kara almost shouted. "She doesn't care about you. All she wants is a soldier to do her bidding."

"I know, and that's what I signed up for," Olivia stated flatly. "Not to get killed, obviously, but I knew what I was getting into when I started working for her. You didn't, and it's my fault you were thrust into this, but you need to accept things the way they are with Vasha, or leave the jobs to me."

Kara nodded. "I got it."

Olivia opened her mouth to say something else, but stopped. "I'm sorry, Kara. I know you're just concerned. I do want your help if you'll stay with me. Together, we're unstoppable."

Kara smiled. "Right," she replied. There was a brief pause before Kara added, "I'm more upset because Vasha's such a bitch."

Olivia's jaw dropped in horror, but it turned into laughter. "Don't say that, she's right in there," she said, pushing her friend. After another moment, Olivia added, "You're right though, she totally is."

The two burst out laughing right in front of the restaurant as passersby gave them wary looks. When they regained composure and self-awareness, they had to catch their breath from laughing so hard.

"Alright," Kara said, "let's find this missing person."

2. SUPERNATURAL EVIDENCE

"So, what should we do first?" Kara asked.

"Well, it would be best to talk with the daughter, as Vasha suggested. She might know something, or be able to give us access to her mother's things."

"No father?"

Olivia opened the file again, holding it against the cold wind outside Vasha's restaurant. "Seems he's estranged. Some kind of deadbeat, so he's not around."

"How are we going to get the daughter to let us inside? We can't very well tell her who we are or who you work for."

"I'll use this," Olivia said as she pulled out her wallet. She opened it to reveal a license with her picture on it and the words 'Private Investigator' on the top.

Kara grabbed it out of Olivia's hands for a closer inspection. "This is so cool, when did you get this?"

"I've had it for a long time. It's an official licence too. It makes my job easier when I can tell people that I'm investigating something. It gives you a lot of access to places that are closed to the public."

Kara handed the license back with a beaming smile of pride aimed at her friend. "I guess you have your shit together."

Olivia laughed. "I like to think so."

Kara and Olivia hailed a cab and went to the address in the file. It was a high-rise luxury apartment. They tried to enter the apartment but the doorman stopped them.

"Excuse me, ladies. Are you here to see someone in the building?"

"Hello, I'm Olivia Lucerno, private investigator," she said, reaching out and shaking the doorman's hand before showing her license.

"We're here to see Stephanie Barker-Wilson about her mother's disappearance."

The doorman leaned in closer to inspect the license, and then nodded. "Such a shame, what happened. Miss Barker-Wilson has been distraught ever since, and can you believe the police think it's a hoax?" He shook his head. "The nerve," he said, folding his arms. "Is she expecting you?"

"No, the research firm Anne works for hired us. We haven't been able to reach Stephanie, but we need her help to begin the investigation."

The doorman nodded. "I'll call ahead then and let her know you're coming."

"Thank you," Olivia replied.

The doorman went up to a terminal beside the door and punched in a few numbers. After a moment, a woman's voice came from the speaker. They talked with each other for a moment.

"That was easy," Kara commented.

"That's usually the easy part. Actually finding who we're looking for can be difficult. With you here, though, we might get a lucky break."

Kara smiled. "The only jobs you've brought me on were boring ones where a psychic owed some money. This one seems pretty exciting."

"Let's hope so," Olivia replied with a stoic expression.

The doorman returned to Olivia and Kara. "Alright ladies, you're welcome to enter. Miss Barker-Wilson will see you."

Olivia nodded. "Apartment three-fourteen, correct?"

"That's correct, miss," he answered as he opened the door for them.

The two of them thanked him and entered the building. The outside spoke to its opulent nature, but the inside was something else. The decorations were lavish and plentiful, with two fireplaces on either side, a dozen expensive recliners and couches, and a large chandelier hanging from the ceiling. A few of the residents were lounging in the chairs, reading.

The Vampire's Rescue

They headed to the elevator and went to the third floor, then went to room three-fourteen at the end of the hall. Olivia took the lead and knocked on the door.

A timid voice came from behind the door. "Who is it?"

"Olivia Lucerno, I'm the private detective the doorman mentioned to you. Could we come in and speak with you, miss?"

The door opened, and in front of them stood a young woman in her late teens by the look of her. Her eyes were red and baggy, and she held a crumpled tissue in her hand. It was evident she was distraught over her mother's disappearance.

"Could I see some identification, please?" she asked.

"Certainly," Olivia said, retrieving her license again.

After a quick inspection, Stephanie moved away from the door to let Kara and Olivia inside. They entered the apartment and removed their shoes.

"Thank you for having us, Miss Barker-Wilson," Olivia said.

Stephanie closed the door behind them and walked towards the living room. "It's just Barker, but call me Stephanie," the girl said with a hint of annoyance. "Follow me."

Olivia and Kara went into the living room and Kara was awestruck. The room was bigger than the apartment she was living in with old Mr. Montgomery. In the centre, there was a sectional sofa facing a picture window affording a beautiful view of the city. In front of the sofa there was a massive square coffee table, and other decorative pieces of furniture were strewn about the living room. Topping it off, there was a fireplace on one side of the living room with a huge television mounted on the wall above it.

"Your mother must be well off," Kara blurted out.

Olivia glanced from Kara to Stephanie. "What my colleague means to say is that your mother must be a respected researcher. What was she studying?" Olivia stared daggers at Kara. She shrugged with an apologetic look.

"Neuroscience," the girl stated simply. "Please, sit." She waved her hand towards the couch. Kara and Olivia took a seat, and Stephanie sat on the other side of the couch near them. "She was researching whether external stimuli can manipulate certain sections of the brain."

Kara and Olivia shared knowing glances. Given their knowledge of Vasha, they could guess the reason she wanted Anne saved.

"I guess the first thing we should ask is if your mother had any rivals or enemies. Anyone at work that she was having issues with or anyone in the industry working on the same research?"

Stephanie looked away in thought. "I work with her most days as an internship for my thesis."

"Your thesis?!" Kara shouted. "How old are you?"

"Nineteen," Stephanie replied. "I graduated high school early and am in my senior year of university."

Kara whistled. "That's impressive. You must be a genius."

Stephanie chuckled softly. "That's what everyone tells me, but I just had a good teacher who pushed me to work hard."

Olivia smiled. "You were saying?"

"Right. I work with my mother, and there aren't many others in our team. Everyone who is loves my mother and looks up to her, as far as I know. When it comes to rivals, there are other people doing similar research with brainwaves, but not the same application as her. Also, her work is independently contracted, so I don't know who would stand to benefit if she was gone."

"Where you here when the kidnapping happened?"

"Yes," she replied. "I was in my room, working on my thesis. I was listening to music when I heard a loud crash like glass breaking. I came out here to see the picture window broken, and when I called for my mother she didn't answer. I went to the window and I could see her being shoved into a van on the other side of the street. I ran outside as fast as I could while I called the police, but the van was gone by the time I got there. I asked people nearby if they saw anything, but it was late at night and there wasn't much traffic at that hour. The doorman is inside at night, so he didn't see anything, and the cameras couldn't see the van."

Olivia peered at the window with a pensive look on her face, and then walked over to it. "Could you point out to me where the van was exactly?"

Stephanie and Kara joined Olivia at the window, and Stephanie pointed a ways down the street. "It was around there."

The Vampire's Rescue

Olivia looked at the wood floor of the apartment, then over at where the van would have been. She stroked the glass of the picture window, deep in thought.

"I had the window replaced this morning," Stephanie commented.

"How did they manage to get her from this floor to the van?" Olivia muttered.

Stephanie's face contorted, like she was in pain. "You don't believe me either, do you?" she whimpered. "Even the police don't believe me. They won't say my mother is missing until more time passes. My mother wouldn't abandon me, not after…" Stephanie pursed her lips. "She wouldn't do that to me," she said, another hint of anger in her voice.

Olivia reached out and touched Stephanie's arm. "I'm sorry, that's not what I meant. I believe that your mother was kidnapped. I'm just trying to figure out how they took her from a third-storey window. Rappelling down from the roof seems like too much work given the height of the building, and taking her from the ground could have injured her."

Stephanie still seemed hesitant about something.

"Please tell us anything you know, Stephanie," Kara encouraged. "It will help us. You can trust us."

Stephanie glanced at the two of them. "Well… we have cameras hidden throughout the house, and several of them showed what happened, but you won't believe it when I show it to you. It's why the police aren't helping me."

"You don't have to worry about that," Kara reassured her. "We've seen our fair share of odd occurrences." Kara glanced at Olivia with a smirk. Olivia chuckled and nodded at Stephanie to affirm their commitment.

Stephanie nodded back, and then walked away. Olivia and Kara followed her into another room which had a computer and other electronics. She went on the computer and opened a folder which had several video files in it. She played one of the videos, and it showed the living room they were just in.

They could see Anne, still wearing her lab coat, talking on a phone in one hand and holding a glass of wine in the other. She was walking around the living room, conversing with a smile on her face. Then she approached the window, and after a minute the window busted open by an invisible force. That same force seemed to pull Anne through the opening. The video was high quality, and they could see out the window the whole time. There were no people rappelling down, nothing which grabbed Anne like rope or anything of the sort, it just looked like she was pulled out as if by the hand of God.

They watched it from a few different angles, but there was nothing new to gain. To Kara and Olivia there was no doubt about what happened: A psychic used telekinesis to pull Anne out of the window.

Kara and Olivia looked at each other with furrowed brows. *Now we know why we're helping a human,* Kara thought.

Stephanie had tears in her eyes. "I wish I had another explanation for what happened, but I don't. Please tell me you're still going to look for her?"

"Of course we are. This just got a whole lot more interesting," Olivia said with an excited smile on her face. "We're going to find your mother and bring her back," she declared.

3. UNDEAD DETECTIVES

"Thank you so much," Stephanie cried.

Kara hugged Stephanie tight. "No tears now, be strong."

Stephanie nodded and wiped her eyes. She pulled away from Kara after another moment and wiped her eyes again. "What will you do now? How will you find my mother?"

"I think the first thing we should do is inspect the location where the van was. There could be a clue left behind," Olivia suggested.

"I checked and didn't see anything, but another pair of eyes can't hurt," Stephanie said with a smile finally on her face.

The three of them exited the apartment and after a few words with the doorman, Stephanie showed Kara and Olivia where she believed the van had been parked. There were a few other vehicles parked in its place now.

"It was somewhere around here. When I checked the other day I couldn't see anything, and before the police saw the video they checked and weren't able to find anything."

Olivia and Kara scoured the area as best as they could between the cars and the pedestrians giving them dirty looks. On the street and the sidewalk there was nothing that they could see which looked out of the ordinary.

Olivia had her brows furrowed and she was glancing around.

"What are you thinking, Olivia?" Kara asked.

"Well, I'm thinking about Anne's phone. From the video we saw, Anne was on a conversation with someone. Did that person contact you, Stephanie?"

"Yes, actually, sorry I didn't think of it before. They said they heard the crash of the window breaking and then my mother screamed. After that she heard some voices telling her to move, and the call cut out soon after that."

"So, she might still have her phone on her. Remember how you found James Moore a few days ago, Kara?"

Kara laughed. "Yeah, but he was taking pictures with GPS on. I doubt Anne's kidnappers would let her take pictures."

"Not likely, but if the GPS is on, and she has service, we might be able to use a find-a-phone feature to track it."

Kara smiled at Stephanie, and she smiled back.

Olivia pulled out her phone and went to a common Find Your Phone page on the internet. "Could you enter your mom's phone number and password?"

"Yeah, luckily she's told me her password in case of emergencies like this. I wish I had thought of this a long time ago."

"It's understandable, you were under a lot of stress," Kara comforted.

Stephanie pulled out her own phone to get her mother's number and punched it into the website, then entered the password. After a moment the next page loaded and she was able to see a general location of where her mother's phone was.

"That's strange," she muttered. "It's showing it right around here."

Kara and Olivia both raised their brows at the same time. "Where could it be?" Kara asked aloud.

Stephanie pulled out her phone and called her mother's. They soon heard a faint ringing noise around them. They starting looking around in tandem, searching for a spot that the phone might have been that they hadn't looked at yet. Almost in unison they looked to the right of the sidewalk, away from the road, and shouted, "The park!"

They all ran inside the park and searched for the noise of the phone. There were a lot of bushes, but the three of them searched through them until they found the phone.

"Got it!" Kara yelled after finding it in the branches of a bush. She pulled herself out of the bush with the hand holding the phone raised triumphantly in the air.

Olivia and Stephanie rushed over to help, and once Kara was upright and cleaned off, they all had smiles on their faces. Kara's smile faded once something dawned on her.

"Wait, how does this help us? Without the GPS pointing us to where they took Dr. Barker-Wilson we won't know where they went."

The Vampire's Rescue

"Well, I'm banking on the thought that she might have been able to take a picture or video of her kidnapping. She's smart, and the phone call seemed to cut off before she was shoved into the van, so it stands to reason that she had enough time to start a recording."

Kara handed the phone to Stephanie, as it was locked. "And if you're wrong?" she asked.

"Well, it's back to square one, then," Olivia replied. "Vasha might be able to pull traffic cam footage though, so we're not totally lost."

"There's a video!" Stephanie exclaimed.

Kara and Olivia leaned in close to watch the video as Stephanie pressed play. They were able to see Anne's bare feet walking along the pavement of the sidewalk. Two sets of voices were giving her orders to keep walking, and after a few seconds the camera turned to show the van in front of her. It was clear from the footage that Anne was trying her best to keep the camera steady. She was able to capture the license plate, but it was partially obscured by one of the kidnappers' legs. After another few seconds, before the back doors of the van were opened, the angle changed and blurred as it was presumably tossed through the air. It landed in the bush they were standing beside, and that was it.

Olivia pulled the video back to where the van's license plate was the most visible, with only two characters missing. "This is great, Stephanie. Your mother is an amazing woman to be able to remain so calm in that kind of a situation. With this, we have a real chance of being able to find her."

Stephanie smiled, tears forming in her eyes again. "I'm so glad."

"I'm going to call Vasha and have her run the plate. She should be able to tell us who it belongs to," Olivia said, pulling out her phone. After a few rings, someone answered. "Hi, this is Olivia, can you send me over to Vasha, please? Thank you." Another few rings and Vasha answered. "Hey Vasha, we have a lead, but we need a partial run through the system. Yeah, it's C, H, T, four, nine, and that's all we have for the plate. White van, two-seater, average size, we weren't able to see any defining features." Kara and Stephanie watched with anticipation as Olivia glanced at them and then off at nothing. After a few moments, and a few vague confirmations from Olivia, she said, "Got it. Thanks, Vasha. We'll handle the rest." Olivia hung up the phone.

"So?" Kara and Stephanie asked in tandem.

"So, the van belongs to a rental dealership. I have the address. We'll have to go there and see if we can get more information on who rented the vehicle."

"Alright, let's go," Stephanie declared.

Olivia and Kara exchanged glances. "I'm sorry, but it's better if you stay here and wait, Stephanie."

Stephanie raised her brow, and then clenched her teeth. "I can't just wait around while my mother is in danger like this. It's going to kill me not knowing if she's safe."

"Chances are it's going to be dangerous. We'll be able to handle it, but you won't."

"You two aren't much older than me," Stephanie said, which produced a laugh from both of them. "And, I've been taking mixed martial arts for years. I can handle myself," she said with confidence.

Kara looked at Olivia and motioned towards Stephanie. Olivia nodded, and then moved like lightning at Stephanie. She used her superior reflexes and strength to flip Stephanie on her back, but made sure to let her down gently. Then Olivia mock punched Stephanie, leaving her fist inches from Stephanie's face.

"No matter how long you've trained for, we've been training longer, and we have the experience to back it up. We can handle this, and we'll bring your mother back to you safe and sound. Trust us," Olivia said.

Stephanie, suspended a foot above the ground by Olivia, nodded. "Alright, I know when I'm beat." Olivia pulled Stephanie back to her feet. "Bring her back, please."

"We will," Kara reassured her.

The three of them went back to the street, and Stephanie stayed to see them off, but before either of them could hail a cab, Stephanie stopped them.

"Don't you have a car?"

"No, neither of us can afford one," Kara replied.

"I wish, it would make things a lot easier," Olivia added.

Stephanie took out her keys and pulled a key off the ring. "Here, take my mother's. I'm only supposed to use it for emergencies, and I think this qualifies."

"Really? That would help us out a lot."

The Vampire's Rescue

"I'll help in any way I can to bring her back," Stephanie replied.

"What about insurance? I don't know how that works. Is it going to be a problem if we borrow the car?"

"It will carry over, and besides, if you bring my mother back I'm sure that she'll cover any repairs."

All three of the ladies laughed. Even in that brief time since they had met Stephanie, Kara and Olivia both felt nice in seeing her smile again, if only for a moment.

They said their goodbyes, and took the car parked in the garage of the apartment building. They travelled to the location that rented the van out. When they arrived, Kara noticed the time.

"Hmm, I hope that we can get the information soon, I need to get back home to make Mr. Montgomery something for supper," Kara said.

Olivia frowned. "That old fart should make his own damn supper."

"You know he can't." Kara had a sad look on her face. "I'm seeing the shadow of death on him more often."

"You said it always goes away, though."

"Yeah, but it didn't use to be this frequent, and each time the visions get more vivid. I don't know why it goes away, but I think he's really going to pass away soon."

Olivia glanced over to Kara, who looked troubled. "You worry too much about everyone. He's too stubborn to die."

Kara smiled. "Thanks."

"Besides, he's food. Don't think of him as your friend."

Kara frowned. "Let's go," she said, releasing her buckle and exiting the car.

They left the car and went inside the rental dealership. Olivia approached the counter. "Hello, an employee of mine rented a van here yesterday, but forgot to bring in the receipt. We kind of need that for tax purposes. Would you be able to print off a copy for me?"

The man at the counter appeared annoyed. "What name was it rented under?"

"Sorry, I don't have the name. I do have the license plate though, will that work?"

The man sighed and rubbed his forehead. "Sure, what's the license plate?" Olivia gave the man the license plate number, and as he entered it into his computer, his expression changed. He seemed to wake up and raised his brow. "Wait, what company did you say you worked for?"

Olivia missed a step. "Uhh, From Dusk Till Dawn Enterprises."

"I'm sorry, but according to my records that vehicle wasn't rented yesterday."

Olivia raised her brow. "I am certain that it was. If you'll please just check your records again. We need that receipt for taxes. It's a business expense."

The man shook his head. "I've already checked, miss. Perhaps it was rented a different day, maybe you should check with your employees. Besides, we can't just give out copies of receipts to anyone, miss. It has personal information attached to it."

Olivia forced a smile and a pleasant tone. "I understand, but I need that receipt."

"Unless you can bring in the person who rented the vehicle so we can sort this out, we won't be able to help you, miss. I'm sorry."

Olivia gritted her teeth. "This is unacceptable. Let me speak to your supervisor."

The man smiled smugly. "I'm the owner," he declared.

Olivia was taken aback. "If you don't resolve this then I'm going to make a complaint to your head office."

The man laughed. "This isn't a franchise, miss. I'm the owner."

Olivia clenched her fist and teeth in a rage. Kara could see what might happen next, and as it was in the middle of the day it was no time for people to see vampires. She grabbed Olivia's arm and tried to take her away from the counter.

Olivia pulled away and pointed at the man and said, "You just lost a customer." She turned around in a huff and walked towards the exit.

"I'm not even sure if you were one," the man muttered.

Kara had to use her psychic powers to keep Olivia from turning around and biting the man's throat. After they left, Olivia let out a muffled scream.

She made a gesture. "I was this close. *This* close!"

"What can we do now?" Kara asked.

Olivia went back to the car to discuss it further. Once the doors were closed she started talking. "We'll have to break in to look over their records."

"Wouldn't it be password protected?"

The Vampire's Rescue

Olivia bit her lip and leaned her head against her hand on the door. "Can you read his mind?"

Kara's eyes widened. "No!" she nearly screamed. "The last time it happened when I was sucking that detective's blood, and I don't know the cause. I have no idea if I'd be able to control it even if I wanted to try. And you know my feelings on draining the living. The only reason I did it the last time was because there was no other way."

Olivia looked away. "I know. I'm sorry. I shouldn't have asked you to do that." Olivia chewed on her thumb. "That guy just pissed me off. I wanted to win."

Kara spaced out for a moment.

Olivia peered at her with a raised brow. "What is it?" she asked.

"I was just thinking how odd it was. He seemed to be working with us at first, but then something happened. Why did he change his attitude?" Kara and Olivia mulled it over for a bit, and then after a moment they both looked at each other and simultaneously said, "The license plate!"

"As soon as we said the license plate number he looked suspicious. Why though?" Olivia pondered.

"He must be in league with the kidnappers," Kara suggested.

"Maybe not directly, but indirectly. He must be supplying the vans to them, but why would he be wary of anyone finding out?"

"It must be because it's off the books. He's not listing the income he's receiving from them because they don't want there to be a record of the rental."

Olivia smiled deviously. "Tax fraud."

"Tax fraud," Kara repeated.

They left the vehicle and went back into the rental dealership. The owner was talking with another employee with a big smile on his face, no doubt retelling how he "humiliated" Olivia. When they approached the desk, he did a double take upon seeing them, but still wore his smirk when he approached the front desk.

"Welcome back, miss," he said with a wide grin. "How can I help you? Have you managed to find the person who rented the vehicle?"

Olivia smiled as well, hiding her fangs, and it threw the owner off. "No, but we can tell you that we have video footage of one of your vans being used to kidnap someone."

The owner lost his smile and sweat appeared on his forehead. "S... So? If anything illegal took place, I can't help that. This is a matter for the police, miss, and I think I'd like you to leave now. I'm going to call them so they can discuss it with you." The owner reached for a phone on one side of the desk.

Olivia leaned forward on the desk and gently placed her hand over the owner's to stop him from making the call. "You wouldn't want to do that," she warned, looking at his name tag. "Greg, let me tell you why you want to work with us. Let's say we do take this to the police. If that vehicle wasn't rented according to your records, and you didn't report it stolen, what do you think will happen? The police will start asking some questions that we both know you don't want raised." The owner gulped. "Give us the information, and we walk away, no more trouble. Or, you can call the police. Your choice." Olivia took her hand off the owner's and folded her arms. Kara did the same, with a big smile directed at Olivia, which she returned.

The owner was sweating, and looked like a deer caught in headlights. He clenched his teeth and gripped the receiver tightly. After a moment, he let go of the phone and his hands fell to his sides. He pulled out a piece of paper and pen, wrote a phone number on it, and then handed it to Olivia.

"This is all I have," he said. "They don't give me any information. All I have is the number they call me on."

Olivia took the paper in hand, glanced at it, and then looked at the owner. "There's nothing else you can give us that will help us find them? What about where they meet to get the vehicles? Have they already returned the van?"

"The van's been returned," he replied, his head hung in shame. "They change the location each time, so it wouldn't help. That's all I have. Please don't call the police," he begged.

Olivia glared at him. "We won't, but you'd better not rent anything to them again, or else."

Olivia and Kara turned around and left the rental dealership. After they exited, they burst out laughing as they walked back to the car. After they entered they were still chuckling and in high spirits.

"Did you see his face? Oh man, that was exhilarating," Kara yelled.

"Yeah, I'm glad we got to stick it to him. What an ass. He knew. He knew right from the beginning we were after him."

The Vampire's Rescue

"But we got him, and now we have another clue."

Olivia pulled out the paper with the number on it. "With this, we can find the people that took Anne."

Kara nodded. "We'll find her, and bring her back to Stephanie." *We'll be back soon, Stephanie. Just hold on a little longer.*

4. FORCE MAJEURE

Olivia called Vasha once again and had her trace the number. The GPS indicated that the phone was on and it was at a vacant office building. The two of them headed straight there, and parked a few blocks away just in case.

"I think we have the right place," Kara stated. "I can feel a lot of psychic energy from that building."

"Good, now I just hope we've made it in time."

"I'm having trouble understanding why they would kidnap or kill Dr. Barker-Wilson in the first place. It seemed like the research could have some sort of repercussion to psychics' brain waves if that was her focus, but according to Stephanie it didn't seem like that's what the research was for. And she was at a loss when it came to what pulled her mother out the window, so she doesn't seem to know psychics are real. Or, at the very least, she doesn't believe in them."

"Maybe they're afraid that someone will point Anne in that direction, and wanted to stop her before that happened? Vasha seems interested in the woman now," Olivia postulated.

Kara scratched her head. "Yes, but that's a result of them kidnapping her, not the other way around. Unless Vasha is the one funding her research?" Kara speculated, looking at Olivia.

Olivia shook her head. "Vasha would have mentioned something if that were the case. If this was an affront to her business, psychics or no, she would rain fire on them to set an example. She wouldn't have just sent me to get the job done."

"Mmm," Kara mumbled. *Why then? Why paint a target on her back to bring Vasha's attention to her?*

The Vampire's Rescue

"It's no use thinking about it right now. The more time we waste, the more time these fuckers have to do whatever it is they want to do."

Kara came out of her thoughts. "Right."

"One thing though, Kara," Olivia started while giving Kara a serious look. "We don't know how many or how powerful these people are, if we're going to do this we have to go for the kill. I'm not saying we *must* kill them, but we can't hold back or hesitate. Are you prepared to do that?"

Kara frowned. "I don't like it, but these people aren't innocent. I won't hesitate when the time comes."

Olivia nodded. "Glad to have you with me, Kara," she said with a smile. "Let's go."

Kara and Olivia left the vehicle and headed down the street towards the building. Kara pulled her hoodie up over her head and covered her face a bit. Olivia was wearing jeans and a loose jacket with a tight t-shirt, so she would stand out no matter what she did. As they approached they could see two men standing outside the door smoking.

The men noticed Olivia and Kara immediately, and began eyeing Olivia, though for a singular reason. "Hey baby, how you doin'?" one of them said, looking her up and down.

"I like that pale skin you got goin' on. You want some colour in you, though?" the second one asked, a lewd look in his eyes.

Olivia didn't miss a beat and sauntered over to them. She let out a girly laugh. "Aww, you guys are sweet. You wanna come back to my place? Me and my friend here will do you right."

The men looked surprised and glanced Kara's way. Kara had trouble acting, so she settled with a smile through her hood and a wave. They grinned ear to ear and became excited like dogs at the sight of a bone.

"You serious, girl?" the first man said.

Olivia chuckled again, and took on a seductive tone. "Of course. We just need a drive and we'll get a party started. You got wheels?"

The two men looked at each other, obviously unable to contain their excitement. They lost all thought of their job to the pull of their loins. "Yeah, we got wheels. Follow us, we'll get you sorted."

They whispered and snickered to each other as they walked down the alley next to the office building. Olivia glanced back at the alley entrance to check if there were any passersby, and once it was clear she nodded at Kara.

Kara focussed her mind, thrust her hands out and slammed them together. As her hands moved, a psychic force slammed the two guys' heads together. It was so sudden there was nothing they could do. They fell to the ground, unconscious.

Olivia picked up the bodies and ran to the other end of the building into a private parking lot. She dumped the bodies next to the back wall of the building one on top of the other.

"So far, so good," Kara commented.

Olivia and Kara examined their surroundings, and noticed an unguarded door at the back for employees. "We can enter the building there. If you see anyone, bind them and I'll handle the rest."

"Got it," Kara replied.

They broke the lock and sneaked into the building, using their fleet feet to avoid making noise. They entered a large open area with elevators on either side and a glass wall separating the front entrance and front desk from the back. Another glass wall on the right led to a dining area with a kitchen. At the front entrance there was a large set of stairs to go to the second floor.

Olivia went to the elevator and tried to push the button, but nothing happened. "Looks like the elevators are busted," She said.

"I can sense two more people on the stairs, but the main energy I'm feeling is on the second floor."

"We'll have to take the stairs then."

They opened the glass door and could hear two people talking above them on the stairs. Olivia motioned for Kara to go on the left side of the stairs, and she was going to take the right.

Kara hunched over as she approached, moving beneath the steps to stay out of sight. She could see two sets of feet, one on either end of the stairs, and she could see her mark leaning against the railing. She looked at Olivia, and Olivia motioned that she was ready.

Kara jumped, reached her arm around her target's neck, pulled him back over the railing to the floor and began choking him. She used her psychic powers to increase her vampire strength. Because he was caught off guard he wasn't able to put up a barrier on his neck to stop her. He struggled psychically and physically against her arm, pulling on it and pushing against it with his hands and mind. She pulled her arm tighter and gritted her teeth as she poured her strength into her choke. Time passed slowly, and every kick of the man's legs and gasp for air was like a slap in her ears. After what felt like an eternity, the man went limp, and Kara loosened her grip. She was breathing through her mouth, sweaty and shaky, but unharmed.

Olivia came over and helped her up. She was also sweaty and breathing hard, but she didn't seem to be shaking from what Kara could tell.

"You alright?" she asked in a whisper.

"Yeah, I wasn't hurt. Are you okay?" Kara asked in return.

"I'm just winded."

Olivia and Kara went around the bottom of the stairs and walked up them in silence. Kara could see the other psychic's body lying prone on the stairs, blood dripping from cuts on his lip and forehead. It looked like Olivia had used her superior strength to punch him until he was knocked out. She watched as Olivia nonchalantly wiped her forehead of sweat while she climbed the stairs.

On the second floor, there were hallways lined with offices on the left and right sides of the building, and another set of elevators in front of them.

"Can you tell who's on this floor?" Olivia whispered.

"No, I just feel a general sense of strong psychic energy. They could be clustered together or suppressing their powers somehow."

"We'll just have to be cautious then."

Olivia moved first, heading to the right side of the building down the hallway of offices. As she moved she first peeked through the windows of each of the offices before passing in front of them. Each of the offices they passed was empty. They went around the corner on the far end, and continued their search.

The hallway they were in now went all the way to the back of the building, and had a fire exit at the far end. It was just empty office after empty office.

"Wait, did you hear that?" Kara said, stopping.

Olivia stopped moving and perked her ears. She pointed to an office a few feet from the fire exit. "There," she exclaimed.

They rushed over to the office with the source of the noise. As they approached, it was clear that the noise was a woman's muffled scream. Olivia went up next to the window of the office and peered inside, then went to the door and opened it.

Inside, Dr. Anne Barker-Wilson was tied to a chair with tape covering her mouth. Her eyes were wide and she was afraid of the newcomers entering the office.

Olivia motioned for Anne to be silent. "We're here to help you," she said.

After a moment, Anne stopped screaming and struggling, and Olivia took the tape off her mouth. "Please help me, these men somehow… they kidnapped me and…"

Kara placed her hand on Anne's shoulder. "It's alright, we know what happened. We're here to rescue you, but in order to get out of here we need you to stay silent," she explained. "Can you do that for me?"

Anne nodded as tears formed in her eyes. "Thank you," she whispered over and over as Olivia removed her bonds.

Once she was freed, Anne stood on trembling feet. "Can you walk?" Kara asked.

Anne nodded. "Yes, I'll be fine. I'm just bit shaken up by all this."

"It's understandable. We'll have you back to your daughter in no time," Olivia reassured her.

"We can use the emergency exit to leave," Kara said.

Olivia left the room, glancing back and forth, but then jumped back into the room and pushed the others in as well. "There's a huge motherfucker at the end of the hall," she exclaimed.

"Shit," Kara replied. "Can we get past him?"

The Vampire's Rescue

"I'm not sure. He was just headed this way when I jumped back in. I think we have to leave now if we're going to do it." Olivia pulled out the key to Stephanie's car and handed them to Anne. Anne raised her brow and looked like she was about to ask a question, but Olivia interrupted. "Your car is outside. Take the key, run out the emergency exit and don't look back. We'll take care of that guy and make sure he doesn't come after you."

Anne shook her head. "I can't do that. I can't just leave you here in my place."

"You don't have to worry about us. We can take care of ourselves. We came here to save you, so let us do our jobs."

Anne looked at the key, then back to Olivia and Kara. She steeled her lips and nodded at them.

Kara and Olivia nodded back, and then ran out of the room. "Run, Anne, run!" Kara screamed.

Anne dashed out of the room and to the fire escape as Kara and Olivia ran towards the psychic in front of them.

Olivia wasn't joking when she said the man was massive. He was over six feet tall and built like a weightlifter or a wrestler. If he also had psychic powers to augment his strength, they would need to work together to take him down.

Kara threw out a psychic blast as they rushed towards him. The man pulled his arms up to block it. The blast made contact, but he was only pushed back a few steps. His lips curled into a devilish smile.

Olivia jumped off the hallway wall and thrust her hand forward, aiming her sharp vampire claws at his neck. He grabbed her hand, spun around, and used her momentum to slam her against the floor. The ground shook with the impact, and it knocked the wind out of her. She coughed and gasped for air.

He's too strong, Kara thought. Olivia's voice sounded in her head. *'Go for the kill.' That's right, I can't afford to hold back, or else we're all dead.*

Kara concentrated on her hands, putting her psychic power behind her fist. She stopped just as she reached the enemy, pivoted on her hips, and threw her best punch at him. It hit him in the back, right at the center of the spine. His back contorted and arched with the punch and he fell to the floor. Kara smiled, proud she was able to hurt him.

Her pride was short-lived, as after he fell to the ground he immediately rolled over onto his back and kicked Kara in the stomach. She doubled over as the blow sent pain throughout her body. The man jumped to his feet, grabbed Kara by the neck, and slammed her to the floor. It took all her willpower just to bring up a barrier, and even then it wasn't enough. Her skull smashed against the carpeted concrete and steel. Her head ached and called out for her to let go of her consciousness.

She fought against the pain and opened her eyes to see the man looming over her. He pressed his burly form against her, and his hand was on her neck and cutting off her air. *I'm sure I hurt him earlier, but he rolled with the punch so it lost all power. If I can just get a clear hit on him…*

Olivia jumped on the man's back, and he let Kara go as he rose to his full height. She was trying to choke him out with her arm wrapped against the tree trunk that was his neck.

Kara coughed to clear her throat, and she struggled for her breath to return as she stumbled to her feet. Olivia was trying her best to knock him out, but he wasn't making it easy. She even tried to bite him right on the cheek and head, but his psychic barrier was too powerful. He was punching her in the face and elbowing her in the ribcage. It wouldn't be long before she would lose her strength.

Kara summoned all her might to her hands, then darted at the psychic. She jumped up, clasped her hands together and threw her hands down at his head.

Before Kara made contact, he dropped to his knees and twisted. Olivia lost her balance on him and her grip on his neck. With those few seconds of weakness, he pulled her off and threw her at Kara. Olivia hit Kara at the center of her mass, and they tumbled backwards.

They tried to get up and regroup, but the psychic wrestler was on them in an instant. He picked up the both of them by their necks with his massive hands and held them in the air. He squeezed on their necks, and they couldn't breathe. The only thing stopping him from crushing their windpipes was their strong vampire bodies.

Kara and Olivia both tried to escape from his grasp, but no matter what they tried it didn't work. They slammed their fists against his arm, pried his fingers, tried to bite him, and kicked him in the chest, but it was all in vain. His long arms meant their kicks didn't reach, and his psychic strength protected his arm and hand.

Kara poured herself into her fists, but it didn't seem to affect him at all. The more she tried, the weaker she became, and she could feel her world going dark. Her eyes became heavier and heavier, and her arms slower and slower. Darkness creeped in from the corners of her eyes.

Liv! her mind screamed. *Stay awake, fight! Fight or Liv dies!* she called out to herself, but her body wouldn't answer. Her arms raised for one last punch, then fell to her side, listless. *Damn it. I wasn't strong enough this time, Liv.* Tears streaked her face; her weakness and failure was the last sting she felt before her eyes closed.

A loud crack brought Kara back to the world of the living, and her eyes sprung open as the constraint around her neck was released. She caught a brief glimpse of Anne standing behind the psychic bodybuilder with a huge fire extinguisher gripped in both hands. Kara fell to the ground, coughing and wheezing. OIivia was in the same condition beside her, grabbing her neck and panting for air.

"Liv! Are you okay?" Kara sputtered out through ragged breaths and a damaged windpipe.

Olivia couldn't stop coughing long enough to answer, but she held her thumb up.

The two of them took another moment to regain their strength, breath, and consciousness. Anne was helping them as best as she could, rubbing their backs and checking their bruised necks. After they were mostly alright, they all rose to their feet.

Olivia moved towards the psychic Anne had knocked out, and she cocked her fist. "No, stop, Liv!" Kara urged in a loud whisper. "We don't have time for this. There could be more of them, and we're in no shape to fight anymore. We need to leave."

Olivia gritted her teeth with her hand still held in the air. After a moment she punched the wall, causing the surroundings to shake. "Tch." She lowered her hand, and the three of them ran to the emergency exit.

"Thanks, Dr. Barker-Wilson, you really saved us back there."

"No problem. I believed you might need help despite what you said, so I located a fire extinguisher and returned as soon as possible. From what I can perceive I arrived just in time."

"You did. Another moment and I don't know what would have happened."

The three women went down the emergency exit and left the building at the side in the middle of the alley. They didn't meet any further resistance as they returned to the car, and, after they piled in, they sped off back to Anne's apartment building.

No one talked for the duration of the car ride. Through the near-death experience and the kidnapping, all three women were still reeling from the trial, and for different reasons.

When they arrived at the apartment, the doorman was shocked and awed to see Anne once again. He was overjoyed, and holding himself back from expressing it. He just kept ushering her into the building telling her to go see her daughter, as well as thanking Olivia and Kara for their good work.

When they got to her apartment, the door opened and Stephanie jumped into her mother's arms with tears streaming down her face. Anne kept stroking her daughter's hair and telling her that it was all right and that she was home safe over and over.

Kara and Olivia both smiled at the sight, and waited for them to finish.

After a moment, Stephanie parted from her mother and rushed over to Kara and Olivia to hug them as well. She pulled them in tight as she bawled her eyes out, babbling thanks again and again into their hair.

They returned the hug, and after another moment they all entered the apartment together to rest. Kara asked for permission to use their kitchen, and she brewed some tea for everyone. While they sipped on the hot minty green tea, they told Stephanie what happened.

First, Anne gave her account of how she was taken and blindfolded until she was brought into the office building. She was isolated and the only times she was visited was to be fed or taken to the bathroom. She attempted escape a few times, and described what Kara and Olivia knew to be psychic occurrences preventing it.

The Vampire's Rescue

Throughout the ordeal, she never learned why they kidnapped her, as no one asked her questions or did anything beyond lock her up.

From there, Kara and Olivia detailed their rescue attempt, glossing over the fact that they used psychic and vampiric powers. After the story was finished, Anne and Stephanie once again thanked them for their help.

"So, we were trying to figure out why you might have been kidnapped, and the only thing we can think of is it somehow relating to your research. Your daughter told us a little bit about what you were doing. Can you think of any reason why someone might have wanted you to stop your research?"

Anne shook her head. "Truthfully, I pondered it quite a bit while I was confined in that room and I wasn't able to come up with a hypothesis."

"Your daughter mentioned you were working on stimulating brainwaves. Can you go into more detail on that?"

"Well, the research is in its infancy, but it's based off of not-so-recent findings from the Allen Institute for Brain Science in Seattle. Scientists were attempting to prove that the claustrum, a particular batch of neurons in the brain, are what holds our conscious thought together. When they stimulated that part of the brain with an electrode, their test subject lost consciousness."

Kara's and Olivia's jaws both dropped. "Just from electric stimulation?"

"That's correct. And my research was to see if there was a way to reproduce the effect externally, without invasive procedures."

"What would be the practical applications of such research?" Olivia asked.

Anne looked away in thought, as if the question had never occurred to her. "Well, I suppose it could help in a number of ways, depending on the end results of my research. If it's only possible with something attached to the body, then it could assist anaesthesiologists during surgery. Having a patient lose consciousness without the use of drugs or invasive technology could save money and aid post-operative care." Anne placed her hand under her chin. "If it is possible to stimulate that part of the brain separate from the body, then it expands the potential indefinitely. Police or the military could use it to control crowds."

"What about stimulating other parts of the brain?" Kara asked.

"I believe we are getting quite ahead of ourselves with this train of thought, but yes, it could be expanded to stimulate other parts of the brain fairly easily, I imagine."

Kara and Olivia looked at each other warily. It was clear now why Vasha had wanted this woman saved and brought to her. She wanted to make a weapon. Kara turned to Olivia, a look of concern on her face. Olivia looked back at her friend with sad eyes, and then she turned away.

"There is something that I need to tell you both," Olivia said.

"Olivia," Kara whispered, "don't."

Olivia ignored her friend. "I said before how we were hired by your research firm, but that wasn't true. We were independently contracted by a woman named Vasha. I work for her, and I believe the reason she wanted us to help you was to offer you a job. She'd like to see you, if you'd be willing to hear out her offer."

Anne looked surprised and glanced at her daughter, then back to Olivia. "Well, I suppose I have her to thank as well. It can't hurt to listen to what she has to say. I owe her that much at least."

"Thank you," Olivia replied. "I understand if you want to rest first, so if you give me your number I'll pass it along to her and she'll contact you at a later time."

"Yes, thank you. That would be best."

Olivia and Anne exchanged information, and after a few more words of thanks, Olivia and Kara left. They went to the elevator and waited for its arrival.

"You didn't have to tell Dr. Barker-Wilson about Vasha. You could have just told Vasha she refused," Kara said.

Olivia stared at her friend. "You know Vasha can see right thought lies, and besides, she would have followed up with Anne anyway."

The elevator came and the two entered it.

"I just can't help but think that we're handing Vasha the tools for a new war," Kara said.

The Vampire's Rescue

Olivia pursed her lips and turned away. She couldn't look her friend in the eyes. "We don't know that. She might want it to empower all vampires for self-defence."

"I guess it's as you always say: we'll cross that bridge when we come to it. There's nothing we can do about it now."

"If we do go to war, Kara, I promise I'll protect you." Olivia stared deep into Kara's eyes and she could see the sincerity reflected in them.

"Same here," Kara replied with a smile.

Olivia pulled Kara in close, and held her hand as they thought on the future, and just what might happen to them if there was another war of psychics versus vampires when one of them was literally caught in the middle.

EPILOGUE

Olivia and Kara entered the small diner called Kalie's together. When they entered, the door struck a bell hanging in front of it and it let out a pleasant tone. The smell of meat and bread cooking wafted up to the both of them as they crossed the threshold.

Olivia had a grin plastered on her face, and when she entered she took in the familiar sights and smells like a child at a theme park. "We're here!" she yelled excitedly, causing the few other patrons to turn their attention to her.

A rotund middle-aged woman ran out of the kitchen, her eyes wide and a curious look on her face. When she saw Olivia and Kara her eyes lit up and she smiled as wide as Olivia. Before she let the smile linger too long, she frowned.

"Where have you two been?" she questioned with her hands at her sides. Her slightly accented voice was motherly, but chastising, like an Italian-American's should be.

Olivia couldn't contain her happiness even to feign shame. "I know, I'm sorry, Kalie. I've wanted to come back for a long time. We're here now, though."

"Tch," she replied. "Ray's in the corner, waiting for you. You want the usuals? Kara?"

"The usual for me," Olivia exclaimed.

"Yes, please," Kara confirmed.

Kalie nodded. "I'll have them out before you can say meatball." She returned to the kitchen.

As Olivia and Kara made their way over to the corner booth that Raymond was sitting in, the other customers said hellos and told them how happy they were to see them again. The few regulars, among whom they used to be included, were like a family unto itself, and like family it didn't matter how much time passed between visits.

The Vampire's Rescue

They sat down in the booth with Raymond, who was huddled in the corner trying to stay unseen. He smiled to them as they joined him. He was wearing a heavy jacket and scarf despite it not being that cold out.

"Sorry we're late, Ray," Kara said.

"It's alright, I wasn't waiting long. Kalie berated me though." Raymond was sweating, but he still smiled.

"At least it's like usual and not crowded."

"Yeah," Raymond replied.

"I'm so excited!" Olivia blurted out.

Kara and Raymond laughed. Olivia was by far the most excited for the food they were about to receive. Kara and Raymond both thought the food at Kalie's was mediocre at best, but it was their usual spot to eat because of the lack of crowds and the atmosphere.

Before long, their food was brought out to them by Kalie herself. "Meatball Sammie for Olivia," Kalie said, handing the plate to Olivia. "Chorizo and bacon pizza for Kara, and salmon and spinach fettuccine for little Raymond," she said with a smile.

Olivia was drooling at the sight of the meatball sub and french fries in front of her. The massive pile of bread, meat, and sauce was steaming, and the smell filled the booth and overpowered the other dishes.

"Well, what are ya waiting for? Dig in!" Kalie commanded.

Olivia went first, and stuffed herself with the sub, her cheeks filling with food like a chipmunk. Kara and Raymond delicately ate their food, watching Olivia scarf hers down with smirks on their faces.

They ate their food, catching up with Kalie and talking with each other about nothing. They laughed as they ate their food, forgetting their troubles if but for a moment.

"It's nice, isn't it?" Olivia asked as she took the last bites of her sub.

Kara took another bite from her pizza. "Yeah, yeah it is."

THE END

THE VAMPIRE'S OMEN

Book 3 of Shawn Wiseman's debut series

PSYCHICS VS. VAMPIRES

Is on sale now through Amazon, Print and Digital.

ABOUT THE AUTHOR

Shawn Wiseman credits his love of reading and writing to his parents, who taught him how to read from an early age, and fostered his creativity.

After almost becoming a boring businessman, Shawn decided to try his hand at writing, and found his passion. He likes strong characters, lots of action, and punchy dialogue. Some of his vices include video games, swearing like a sailor, and fast food.

Shawn gets inspiration from his friends and family who continue to encourage him with his writing. Before trying his hand at self-publishing, a friend was the one who convinced him to try a writing challenge, and he hasn't looked back since then. His biggest goal is to create characters and stories that will inspire others to try their hand at writing, just as he was inspired before.

It would help Shawn out if you shared this novel with your friends or leave a review on Amazon.